Dear Parent:
Your child's love of reading starts here!

Every child learns to read in a different way and at his or her own speed. Some go back and forth between reading levels and read favorite books again and again. Others read through each level in order. You can help your young reader improve and become more confident by encouraging his or her own interests and abilities. From books your child reads with you to the first books he or she reads alone, there are I Can Read Books for every stage of reading:

SHARED READING
Basic language, word repetition, and whimsical illustrations, ideal for sharing with your emergent reader

BEGINNING READING
Short sentences, familiar words, and simple concepts for children eager to read on their own

READING WITH HELP
Engaging stories, longer sentences, and language play for developing readers

READING ALONE
Complex plots, challenging vocabulary, and high-interest topics for the independent reader

I Can Read Books have introduced children to the joy of reading since 1957. Featuring award-winning authors and illustrators and a fabulous cast of beloved characters, I Can Read Books set the standard for beginning readers.

A lifetime of discovery begins with the magical words **"I Can Read!"**

Visit www.icanread.com for information
on enriching your child's reading experience.

Library of Congress Control Number: 2021936537
ISBN 978-0-06-303746-5

Book design by Elaine Lopez-Levine

21 22 23 24 25 LSCC 10 9 8 7 6 5 4 3 2 1 ❖ First Edition

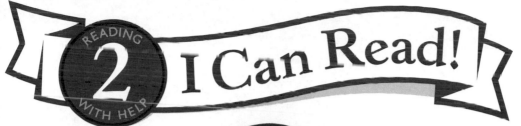

I Can Read!

Reading 2 With Help

PONIES UNITE

Adapted by
Megan Roth

HARPER
An Imprint of HarperCollins Publishers

Meet five new pony friends!

They hope for a better world.

Did you know that all ponies
can make a difference?
Ponies are stronger together.

Long ago in Equestria,

all the ponies lived together.

Now, Earth ponies live by the bay.

Pegasus ponies live up high.

Unicorns live in the woods.

Meet Sunny Starscout.

She is an Earth pony.

Everypony loves Sunny's smoothies.

Smoothie deliveries are fun
when you're rollerblading!

Sunny is a dreamer.

Her dream is to meet a Unicorn

or maybe even a Pegasus.

Sunny wants to show everypony
the magic of friendship.

Sunny loves adventure.

She stands up for what is right.

Bringing back harmony

is the right thing to do.

That is Sunny's mission!

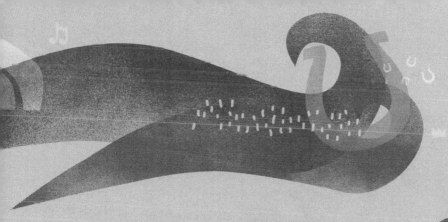

Meet Izzy Moonbow.

Izzy is a Unicorn.

Her high energy helps her

do all sorts of things.

When Izzy gets inspired,

there's no telling what she can do!

Izzy is very creative.

She is great at crafts,

especially crafts that use glitter!

Izzy makes friendship bracelets.

She wears her favorite one.

It has blue, purple, and green beads.

17

Izzy is very caring.

She is a really good friend.

Sunny is Izzy's best friend.

Meet Princess Pipp Petals.

She is a Pegasus.

This royal pop star has a lot
of fans on social media!

Pipp is very glamorous
and full of joy.
The world is her stage.
She wants to fill it with music.
She wants to make the world happier.

Meet Princess Zipp Storm.

She is a Pegasus, too.

Her twin sister is Pipp Petals.

Zipp is a royal rebel.

She takes risks.

She's a super cool pony.

Zipp is completely fearless.

She is a master secret keeper.

She is very loyal.

She always helps her friends.

Meet Hitch Trailblazer.

He is an Earth pony.

He is the town sheriff.

He works with his deputy, Sprout.

Critters follow Hitch everywhere.

They know he will protect them.

Hitch is very brave.

He keeps everypony safe.

He cares about all ponies,
especially his friends.

These ponies are on a mission.
Together there is nothing
these friends can't do.